The Secret Fairy in Fairyland

To J.D. with love
—Penny Dann

To Mum, my best friend
—Claire Freedman

Text copyright © 2001 by Claire Freedman
Illustrations copyright © by Penny Dann

First American edition 2002 published by Orchard Books
First published in Great Britain in 2001 by Orchard Books London
Claire Freedan and Penny Dann reserve the right to be identified as the author
and the illustrator of this book. SECRET FAIRY and the SECRET FAIRY
Device are the trademarks of Orchard Books, London

ISBN 0-439-35240-1   LC data available.
10 9 8 7 6 5 4 3 2 1   02 03 04 05

Printed in Singapore

First edition, September 2002

The Secret Fairy in Fairyland

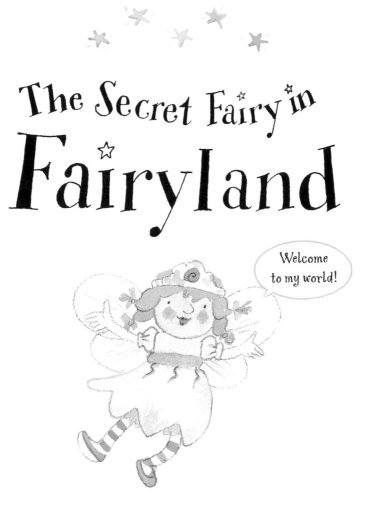

Welcome to my world!

As told by the Fairies to
Penny Dann and Claire Freedman

ORCHARD BOOKS • NEW YORK
An Imprint of Scholastic Inc.

✷ Contents ✷

✶ Welcome to Fairyland ✶

Hi, Secret Fairy
fans! Come visit Fairyland and
meet all my best fairy friends.
It's great fun here — there are always lots
of parties to attend and fairy work to
be done. Fairyland is a
very busy place!

I'm
Nettle. I'm Blossom's
special best friend. She
says I'm great fun to be
with because I get into all
kinds of mischief.
Oops!

Hello! I'm
Bluebell, and at my hair
and beauty parlor Blossom and
all the fairies share their
secrets with me!

Buzz!

✲ Blossom and the Missing Necklace ✲

One spring day, Blossom was out walking when she came across a fairy flower trail.

Who has left this?

I wonder who's in there. Hello?

Blossom excitedly followed the trail. It led to a secret door in the palace.

I really need your help.

DANCING COMPETITION
* * *
the best dancer will be awarded the Fairy Queen's SURPRISE PRIZE!

I'll do my best, Your Majesty.

Inside, Blossom found the Fairy Queen. She seemed upset and explained that she had lost a special necklace, which was to be awarded at the Fairy Dancing Competition that afternoon.

Blossom agreed to help. She would make a new necklace so no one would know.

"Good luck, Blossom. And thank you."

"Don't worry. Your secret is safe — I won't even tell Nettle."

"I must find something even prettier."

Back at her boutique Blossom searched through her fairy jewels. None looked quite right.

"Here you are, Blossom."

"One of every color!"

"We're always happy to help!"

"It's perfect, thank you!"

Blossom decided to visit the treetops. The birds gave her some feathers, and the friendly ladybugs helped string the feathers together.

"This should do the trick!"

"A masterpiece!"

"Yoo-hoo! Blossom!"

"We've come to call for you!"

"Oh, no! They mustn't see the necklace!"

At the boutique Blossom sprinkled the necklace with fairy dust. Now it really glittered!

Blossom had forgotten that Nettle and Bluebell were picking her up on their way to the dance.

Nettle and Bluebell couldn't understand why Blossom wasn't ready to go.

After her friends had left, Blossom tidied up a little and then put on her party dress.

It wasn't until she was leaving for the dancing competition that Blossom remembered the necklace. But where had she put it? She searched everywhere. . . .

Blossom rushed to the palace as fast as she could to explain to the queen that she had lost the second necklace!

Lovely necklace, Blossom, but we don't want the others to see it!

Errr, I didn't have anything to carry it in!

Gibbering gemstones — I'm wearing it!

Oh, Blossom, the necklace is marvelous!

Blossom quickly took the necklace off and handed it to the Queen.

Ha-ha! Well done!

Bravo, Blossom!

What a lovely necklace!

She's a great dancer!

Blossom relaxed and really enjoyed the dancing. But both Blossom and the queen laughed out loud when the winner was announced! And of course, Blossom pretended to be surprised when the Fairy Queen handed her the prize necklace!

✳ Fairyland Jewelry ✳

Glitterbug Feather Necklace

You will need: Three feathers
Thin colored cardboard · A penny
Pencil · Scissors · Clear glue
A length of cord long enough to fit over
your head · Fairyland stickers

1. Fold the cardboard in half. Place the penny so that it extends over the fold and draw around it. Do this three times. Cut these cardboard beads out but don't cut through the folded spines.

2. Find the middle of your length of cord and hang a cardboard bead over it. Apply glue to the inside of the bead and press the sticky sides together to hold the bead in place on the cord.

3. Hang two beads, evenly spaced, on either side of the center bead. Glue them onto the cord in the same way and allow the glue to dry.

3. glitterbug sticker

2. feather

1. glue

4. Glue a feather on top of each bead so that it hangs down. Allow the glue to dry and add a glitterbug sticker to each feather, as shown.

Glitterbug Feather Brooch

Now cut out a single circle shape
from the cardboard using a penny.
Decorate it in the same way.
Attach a safety pin to the back of
the brooch with a small piece
of sticky tape — watch your fingers!

Sparkle Rings and Spangly Bangles

For the rings:

1. Cut a piece of cardboard about ¹/2 inch by 2 ¹/2 inches Overlap
and glue together the edges to make a ring that will fit on your
finger.

2. Allow the glue to dry before
sticking sparkling Fairyland
stickers all around the ring.

For the bangles:

1. Cut a piece of
cardboard about
1 ¹/2 inch by 8
inches. Cut a
wiggly shape
along both
edges. Overlap
and glue the
ends to make a
bangle that fits
over your hand.

2. Decorate the bangle with beautiful spangly
stickers.

Fairy Fashion Parade

Spring and Summer Surprises

My friend Rosebud and the fashion fairies sew flower petals together to make fairy dresses. Rosebud has invited us all to the Summer Fairy Fashion Parade.

Gasp!

Oh, my!

I'd like that one!

That is lovely!

It looks as though the fashion fairies have thought of everything for summer! Don't you love those stripy beach towels made from green moss and marigold petals? Take a look at the starfish flip-flops too! Now all the fairies can sunbathe on the beach in style! Hurry up — vacation time!

Wow, rainbow dresses!

How exciting!

I love the "sea urchin" look!

Don't trip in those shoes!

Look this way, please!

⋆ The Clumsy Fairy ⋆

It was almost time for Fairyland's May Ball. All the fairies were excitedly discussing what to wear.

"I wonder who will be crowned May Princess this year," Blossom said.

"Well, it won't be me!" joked Hollyhock. "I'm so clumsy I'd probably drop the crown and break it!"

The other fairies all giggled at this. It was true — Hollyhock was a very clumsy and messy fairy. But she was so friendly and funny, it didn't matter a bit, and everyone loved her.

On the morning of the ball, Hollyhock was flying in the woods. She was looking for some petals to make into a necklace, but some pretty flowers caught her eye. Hollyhock flew down to look at them. She didn't notice an old tree stump and crashed straight into it!

"Clumsy me!" she cried. "Now I've got moss stains on my skirt, and I've squashed the primroses!"

As Hollyhock brushed herself off, she saw something glinting among the leaves below. She flew down and picked it up. It was a lovely, sparkly pin.

"This belongs to Rosebud, the fashion fairy," Hollyhock said. "It's been missing for ages. Oh, she will be pleased I've found it."

Hollyhock rushed over to see Rosebud at once. She found her busily adding the final touches to the Fairy Queen's beautiful ball gown. Rosebud was delighted to have her brooch back.

"It's great to see that you found it," she told Hollyhock. "Now I can wear it to the ball tonight. Is there anything I can do to thank you?" she asked.

Hollyhock hesitated.

"I wonder, could you make *me* look wonderful for the ball?" she asked hopefully. "However hard I try, I always end up looking like a silly mess!"

"No problem!" Rosebud replied. "I'm not Fairyland's top fashion fairy for nothing. We'll get to work at once!"

What an afternoon Hollyhock had! While one fairy styled her hair, others worked on her makeup and dress. At long last she was ready for the ball.

"Oooh!" Hollyhock gasped in amazement as she stared at her reflection in the mirror. "I don't look like me anymore. I look like a . . . princess!"

"It's a lovely dress," Rosebud said. "Pink and purple with lilac shoes and a bag to match."

"My face looks so different too," Hollyhock said with delight.

"It's the rainbow makeup," Rosebud replied. "Wait. You need one final touch!" And she sprayed Hollyhock with the most gorgeous perfume.

Hollyhock arrived at the ball wondering what her friends might say when they saw her.

"They probably won't even recognize me," she thought. And no one did!

"Hello, Blossom! Hi, Bluebell!" Hollyhock called. "Surprise — it's me!" But the music was so loud they couldn't hear her and just wondered who she was.

Feeling disappointed, Hollyhock decided to find something to eat. The food looked delicious, and she was just about to take a huge bite of strawberry cake when she had a worrying thought.

"Knowing me, I'll spill food down my dress and spoil it," she sighed. She put down the cake and headed for the dance floor instead. It was crowded with fairies whirling and swirling about. Hollyhock longed to join in, but she knew what would happen if she did. She'd trip over someone's feet and end up breaking the heel of her shoe. So Hollyhock sat in a corner feeling glum, watching the other fairies enjoy themselves. Suddenly she made a decision.

She rushed home, changed into her red
dress, and washed off some of the makeup!

"Now I look and feel like me again,"
she said. "And I can have some fun!"

In no time Hollyhock was back at the ball.

"At last — you're here!" called Blossom.

"We missed you!" Bluebell said. "Never mind.
You're just in time to hear who has been chosen as
the May Princess."

Everyone hushed as the Fairy Queen announced the winner — Hollyhock!

"Me?" gasped Hollyhock, knocking over a table as she rushed to receive her
crown from the Fairy Queen. "But I'm such a hopelessly clumsy fairy."

"And a very nice one, too," the Fairy Queen said as everyone clapped.
Happily, Hollyhock helped herself to some strawberry cake. And when she
accidentally bumped into another fairy and sent the crown flying into the jelly,
even the Fairy Queen laughed!

✴ Ballet with Blossom ✴

Welcome to your first fairy ballet class. Hollyhock and Blossom are going to show you some basic ballet steps.

Bluebell is playing the music for us on the piano. Music, Maestro!

1. Begin with your legs and feet turned out. Stand with both heels together and turn out your feet so your toes point outward. This is called *first position*.

This is not right!

2. Now place your feet apart, like this. Keep your feet and toes turned out. This is called *second position*.

Tut, tut!

BUMP!

3. Next cross the heel of one foot halfway in front of the middle of the other foot. Remember to stand up straight and keep your feet turned outward. This is *third position*.

It helps to wear clothes you can easily move in, like a leotard or leggings. Wear soft shoes or go barefoot. Tie your hair up, too.

4. Dancers need good balance. Try to stand still on one foot without wobbling. Remember to keep pointing your toes and feet. Hollyhock is steadying herself on a chair for this exercise.

Mmm...

Oops, I nearly did a split!

5. Now try this well-known position called an *arabesque*. Balance on one leg with your other leg stretched out behind you. Hold your arms out gracefully.

Careful, Hollyhock! I think your shoes are untied.

Whoa! I don't feel so well!

6. Make up a dance using all these different positions. Finish with a twirl, called a *pirouette*. Spin around as fast as you can. Well done. Take a bow!

I did tell her!

✳ Fairyland Friends ✳

Introduced by Lavender and her insect friends

We share our lives with our animal neighbors. They help us with the day-to-day running of Fairyland.

Let us all count together. One leg, two legs . . .

The centipedes and millipedes help out at Fairyland School. They're very handy for teaching the little fairies how to count.

The Fairy Queen's bees are busy all summer long. They collect sweet nectar from the flowers to make into delicious honey.

The fashion fairies follow the bees wherever they go! That's how they know where to find the prettiest petals for their fairy dresses.

Cake crumbs!

The ants keep Fairyland clean and tidy. Every evening they gather up the crumbs from parties and picnics. The goodies are marched back to the ants' nest for supper!

The ladybugs and caterpillars string dewdrops and berries onto blades of grass to make necklaces and dangly earrings for Blossom's Boutique.

Blossom's Boutique

It's beautiful!

For you!

The Chirping Crickets are a favorite bug band. All the fairies enjoy listening to the wonderful music they make!

Spiders are useful, too. They catch tiny dewdrops in their webs. Then the raindrop fairies collect the delicate dewdrops in acorn cups.

Take your partners for the butterfly waltz.

Dance School

Everyone in Fairyland loves to dance. So the butterflies run their famous Flutterby Dance School. Lessons are held every day in the Fairy Queen's palace ballroom.

★ Are You Animal Friendly? ★

Do you love animals? Would you know what to do in a creature crisis? Try my quiz to find out how animal friendly you really are. On a piece of paper, write down each answer you would choose.

1. You're watering the Fairyland vegetable garden when you spot a new rabbit hole close by. Do you:

A) Get annoyed! Those rabbits will munch through your vegetables in no time!

B) Feel pleased — and hope to spot some baby bunnies.

C) Leave out a few carrots for the rabbits to eat.

Yap!

2. You'd love a little puppy, but you work in the perfume factory all day, and there's no one at home to take care of him. Would you:

A) Get a puppy anyway — and leave him alone all day.

B) Have fun walking your neighbor's little dog each evening.

C) Settle for a goldfish.

3. The Fairy Queen asks you to look after the hedgehogs living at the bottom of the palace gardens. Do you:

A) Give the hedgehogs some leftovers from your tea.

B) Leave them water and a plate of dog food.

C) Leave out some bread and milk.

4. While walking in Fairyland woods, you spot two blackbirds building their nest. Would you:

A) Take the nest home with you to show your friends.

B) Watch quietly from a distance — you don't want to disturb the birds.

C) Climb the tree for a better look.

Oooh, what a beautiful starfish!

5. You're on vacation at the seashore, and find a beautiful starfish in a rock pool. What do you do?

A) Take it home — it would look great in your aquarium.

B) Admire the starfish — but don't touch it.

C) Carry it inside and try to feed it.

How did you score?

Mostly A
Sometimes you seem to forget that animals have feelings, too! Try spending more time observing animals and their needs. You'll understand the importance of being kind.

Mostly B
You are a real animal lover. You know exactly how to care for creatures big and small. Keep it up and you'll be every animal's friend.

Mostly C
You like animals and try hard to help them. You still have a little more to learn about caring for them, but you're on the right track!

Strawberry Ladybugs

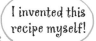

You will need:
Large strawberries
A bar of chocolate
Waxed paper
A small clean paintbrush
One large and one small heat-proof bowl

1. Carefully remove the stems from the strawberries. Cut them in half and lay them flat side down on a sheet of waxed paper.

2. Break the chocolate into a small bowl. Place the small bowl inside the larger bowl and ask an adult to pour boiling water in between the two, halfway up the side. Let sit for five minutes and then carefully remove the small bowl. Stir the chocolate with a spoon.

3. Dip the tip of each strawberry half into the melted chocolate to make the ladybug's head. Lay flat side down on the waxed paper to dry.

4. Use the brush to paint on chocolate wings and spots. Allow the chocolate to set.

Hello?

Blossom's Tip

Try making chocolate rose leaves. Dip the shiny side of clean rose leaves into the melted chocolate. Let sit to harden and then peel off!

More tea, Violet?

5. Arrange the ladybugs and leaves on a pretty plate and share with friends!

✦ Blossom's Seashore Surprise ✦

Blossom and her friends have been having a great seashore vacation. But the week is nearly over.

Let's hold a farewell beach party!

I don't want to go home.

The next day the fairies began to get everything ready for their beach party.

I'm decorating the party area with flowers.

I'll prepare the food.

What else will we need?

Why not organize the entertainment?

Everyone was busy except for Blossom. For once, she couldn't think how to help.

Blossom walked along the beach, trying to plan some party games. Suddenly she heard the most beautiful singing!

Who's that singing?

To Blossom's surprise it was a mermaid! She smiled at Blossom and said that her name was Coral.

What a lovely voice you have.

Thank you. I do it all the time — I love to sing!

When Coral heard about the fairies' party, she had an idea for the entertainment.

I'd like to sing for you all at the party.

Gosh, would you?

What fun this will be!

Tee-hee! I'll hide here until you call my name!

Blossom and Coral arrived back at the beach as the party was about to begin.

A mermaid!

Clever Blossom!

Sing us another song, Coral!

Hurrah!

Three cheers for Coral!

As soon as everyone had eaten, Blossom sat them down and called to Coral. The other fairies could hardly believe it, and they loved Coral's singing!

★ Perfect Party Tiara ★

Make my Secret Fairy tiara and crown yourself Sea Queen!

You will need:

A tape measure ✷ A large silver or gold cake doily about 8 inches across
Thin silver or gold cardboard ✷ Clear glue ✷ Scissors ✷ Fairyland stickers

1. First make the headband. Measure around your head and add on 1¹/2 inches. Cut out a strip of colored cardboard 1 inch wide to the length of the above measurement. Overlap the ends by 1¹/2 inches and glue them together to make the base of your tiara. Allow the glue to dry.

2. Make a fold across the doily about 3 inches deep. Cut across the fold.

3. Apply glue along the back of the piece of doily and attach it to the front of the headband.

4. Find the spangly seashells among the Fairyland stickers and stick them all over the tiara to decorate it.

✳ Hair and Beauty Secrets ✳

From Bluebell's Beauty Parlor

Wheee!

Bluebell is a very talented hairstylist. Fairies come from far and wide to have their hair done here. I've asked Bluebell to show you how to make some of her beautiful hair creations. Hollyhock, Nettle and I are going to be Bluebell's models — what fun!

For these hairstyles you will use:

A brush ✳ Ribbons ✳ Bobby pins ✳ A mirror ✳ Small ponytail holders ✳ A comb
Brush your hair smoothly before you start each style.

We've used ribbons in two different colors.

Beauty Bows
modeled by Nettle

You will need:

4 lengths of narrow ribbon
(each 10 inches long) ✳ 4 bobby pins

1. Tie a knot in the middle of each piece of ribbon.
2. Slide a bobby pin through the back of each knot.
3. Tie a bow on top of each knot.
4. Brush your hair and use the comb to make a center part.
5. Put two bows on each side of your hair, just above your ears.

This hairstyle is easy to do!

This looks great on long hair.

Bunches of Fun
modeled by Hollyhock

You will need:

2 pieces of narrow ribbon
(twice the length of your hair),
4 small, matching ponytail holders

1. Take the comb and make a middle part down the back of your head. Gather each side into a bunch and secure each bunch at the top and bottom with the ponytail holders.
2. Loop a ribbon through one of the top holders. Pull it through to make equal lengths on both sides.
3. Twist the ribbons around and around the bunch, crossing the ribbons over each other as you go. Knot the ribbon ends into a bow at the bottom ponytail holders.

Bunches 'n' Scrunchies
modeled by Blossom

You will need:

4 small ponytail holders ⋆ 4 lengths of narrow ribbon (each 10 inches long)

1. Divide your hair into a middle part again with the comb.
2. Keep one half out of the way with a ponytail holder.
3. With your comb make another part down the center of the loose hair. Secure each section with a ponytail holder.
4. Tie bows over these two ponytail holders using the ribbons.
5. Repeat on the hair on the other side of your head.

Wear your special Fairyland nail tattoo stickers to add the finishing touch!

This is such a cute hairstyle!

Fizzy Fairy Pop

Bluebell serves these refreshing drinks in her beauty parlor. I like sipping them while I'm having my hair done! Each recipe serves four fairies.

Fizzy Fairy Floats

You will need: A bottle of cherry soda * Vanilla ice cream
Colored sugar sprinkles * Glasses * Straws

1. Fill each glass three-quarters full of cherry soda.

2. Add a scoop of vanilla ice cream to each glass.

3. Drop lots of colored sugar sprinkles over the ice cream.

Droool! I'm feeling rather thirsty, Bluebell.

4. Top with a straw and serve at once.

Long Green Fairy Fizz

You will need: A bottle of lemonade * Lime juice
Green food coloring * 2 kiwifruits * Glasses * Straws

1. Peel and slice the kiwifruits. Put a few slices into each glass.

2. Pour a little lime juice and a drop of the food coloring into each glass.

3. Fill up the glasses with lemonade. Add a straw to each. Then serve and slurp!

Party Umbrella

You will need: Pretty paper cake cups
Modeling clay * Popsicle sticks * Sticky tape * Scissors

Bluebell tops her fairy fizz drinks with a pretty umbrella.

1. Gently flatten a cake cup a little with your palm and cut a triangle out of the circle of paper, as shown.

2. Overlap the cut edges and tape them together, putting tape on both sides of the paper umbrella.

3. Push a popsicle stick through the center of the umbrella and out the other side, into a ball of modeling clay.

Look under your birthday month to discover your secret fairy jewel sign.

⋆ Fairy Horoscopes ⋆

Written by Mystic Moth

January Fairy Jewel — Garnet

Garnet fairies are confident and love adventure. They make great leaders (the Fairy Queen is a Garnet). Garnet fairies like to keep busy all day long — but they must try not to rush into things too quickly.

February Fairy Jewel — Amethyst

Amethyst fairies make very good and loyal friends. They love pretty things and dressing up in beautiful clothes. Amethyst fairies are also good at sharing with other fairies. They can be a bit scared of taking risks at times.

March Fairy Jewel — Aquamarine

Aquamarine fairies are very easygoing and are fun to be with. They feel happiest out of doors in the countryside. Aquamarine fairies can be terrible timekeepers and often arrive late at parties but make up for it once they arrive.

April Fairy Jewel — Diamond

Diamond fairies are home-loving and often make wonderful cooks. They prefer to spend a quiet night in rather than going to a noisy party. Diamond fairies like to have one special close friend (usually another Diamond fairy!).

May Fairy Jewel — Emerald

Emerald fairies always look neat and love tidying things up! They are dainty and graceful and are often good at dancing. Emerald fairies can sometimes be a little bit shy about meeting new people — but are always liked by everyone.

June Fairy Jewel — Pearl

Parties are Pearl fairies' favorite times. They are often good singers or actors and enjoy performing for their friends. Pearl fairies like to be in the center of a crowd and are great at organizing events. They must try not to be too bossy.

What do you call a fairy with a daisy in each ear? Anything you like — she can't hear you!

July Fairy Jewel — Ruby

Ruby fairies are full of fun! They are always giggling with friends and telling silly jokes. They are also good at explaining ideas to other fairies. Ruby fairies have only one fault — they are nonstop chatterboxes!

August Fairy Jewel — Peridot

Peridot fairies are adventurous. They enjoy climbing trees, cycling on their bikes, and exploring exciting new places. Peridot fairies love animals of every kind and tend to keep lots of pets. They can be rather messy fairies and hate cleaning up!

September Fairy Jewel — Sapphire

Sapphire fairies are very artistic. They like to paint and are clever at sewing and making their own clothes. Because they are such good listeners, they have plenty of friends. But don't ask one for advice — Sapphire fairies can never make their minds up about anything!

October Fairy Jewel — Opal

Opal fairies are sporty types. They are enthusiastic about everything they do and are full of good ideas. When they're not playing games, Opal fairies often have their nose in a good book. Opal fairies must try to remember to share more with their friends.

ovember Fairy Jewel — Yellow Topaz

Yellow Topaz fairies are always happy and cheerful. They are big nature lovers. If they find an injured animal, you can bet they'll want to care for it. They never forget to leave food out for the birds in winter. Yellow Topaz fairies must remember to look after themselves, too!

December Fairy Jewel — Blue Topaz

Blue Topaz fairies are usually very clever. They learn new things quickly and have good memories. Blue Topaz fairies like to find out how everything works and enjoy puzzles and quizzes. They often don't like getting up in the mornings!

* The Fairy Fashion Show *

There is a lot of excitement among the fairies.
There's a new fashion show coming to Fairyland!

I can't wait!

the Fashion Fairies present A FASHION PARADE next weekend 6pm

I wonder if I could help?

I could be a model!

Blossom visited the fashion fairies in their secret underground burrow. They were busily sewing outfits for the show.

This is our showroom.

Oooh, what gorgeous clothes!

You'd look good in this!

I'd love to be a model!

Blossom kindly offered to help out. To her delight, Rosebud, the fashion fairy, said she could model some clothes!

There was plenty to do before the show! Bluebell braided Blossom's hair with flowers and fixed her makeup.

Blossom felt very nervous as the music began and she stepped out onto the stage!

The fashion show was a great success! Blossom didn't make one wrong step as she paraded in the fabulous clothes.

Blossom modeled the most beautiful dress of all. When the show ended, she didn't want to take it off!

But Rosebud gave Blossom the dress as a "thank you" present for all her help!

✶ Blossom and the Dragonfly ✶

It had been a morning of sunshine and showers. Now it was dry again. Blossom, Nettle, and Bluebell were playing outside. They were happily leapfrogging over red-spotted toadstools when the Fairy Queen passed by in her carriage.

"Fairies!" the queen called out. "I've got a very special job for you to do. Because of the weather, we've had lots of rainbows today. I was hoping you could

Thank you, fairies!

collect the gold fairy dust from the ends of the rainbows." The Fairy Queen handed Blossom a big basket to collect the gold fairy dust in.

"See you later." She waved as her carriage headed off in the direction of the palace.

Blossom and her friends set off excitedly. Looking for the glittering gold fairy dust was a favorite task!

"Here's some!" Nettle shouted a little later. "Oooh, it's *sooo* pretty!"

"You're supposed to put the gold dust in the basket — not all over yourself!" Bluebell giggled.

Before long the basket was almost full when they heard a cry.

"Help, help!"

"Stop singing so loudly, Nettle!" Blossom shushed. "I can hear someone in trouble."

The fairies found a large dragonfly trapped in a bramble bush.

"Don't wriggle," Bluebell told the dragonfly as she struggled to free it.

Will it hurt?

"Thank you," the dragonfly replied gratefully. "But, oh dear, look at my poor torn wing. The brambles have completely ruined it."

The fairies stared at the broken wing in dismay.

"I know," said Bluebell. "I'm good at sewing. I'll weave a new wing using silken threads from a spider's web."

With Spidey's kind help Bluebell had soon finished stitching the wing.

"There! It doesn't look bad."

The dragonfly flapped his wing gently to try it out.

"It works perfectly," he said, darting here and there. "But it doesn't shimmer and glint in the light as my old wing did."

The fairies had to agree the new wing looked a little dull. But no one could think of how to make it shimmery again.

"The Fairy Queen might have an idea," Blossom told the dragonfly brightly. "Why don't you come back to the palace with us?"

The dragonfly had never been inside the
palace before. As the footman showed
them in, all the fairies curtsied and
presented the Fairy Queen with the
basket full of gold fairy dust.

Well done!

"Please, Your Majesty, here is your basket," said Blossom proudly.
Then she explained what had happened to the dragonfly.
The Fairy Queen laughed.

"You are holding what you need to help
the poor dragonfly," she said with a smile.
And she reached into the basket and took
out a handful of the sparkly gold dust.

The moment she sprinkled it over
the dragonfly's wing, it shimmered
and glinted — just as it should!

Thank you,
fairy friends.

What Kind of Fairy Are You?

If you lived in Fairyland, what sort of fairy would you be? Try our quiz and find out. On a piece of paper, write each answer you would choose.

1. The perfume fairies ask you to test their new scent. It smells terrible! What do you do?
A) Be honest and then spend all day helping them brew up a new mixture.
B) Hold your nose and pretend to faint!
C) Say you love it — you don't want to hurt their feelings.

2. A small fairy asks to use your new glitter makeup. Do you:
A) Say yes and ask if you can borrow her sparkly barrettes.
B) Tell her no. You're fed up with other fairies using your stuff.
C) Say yes and kindly offer to show her how to wear it best.

3. You've been invited to the Fairy May Ball and can't afford to buy a new dress. What do you do?
A) Sew ribbons and sequins onto an old dress and make it look as good as new.
B) Stay at home.
C) Go and enjoy yourself anyway — it doesn't really matter what you wear.

4. Your best fairy friend tells you she's moving to another Fairyland on the other side of the world. Would you:

A) Look forward to receiving lots of interesting postcards from her.

B) Drop your friend immediately and start looking for a new best friend.

C) Give her a wonderful going-away party.

Oh, no! I've forgotten Jason's birthday!

5. It's your little elf brother's birthday, and you've forgotten to buy him a present. Would you:

A) Pretend you're giving him a surprise later and rush out to buy something.

B) Find an old toy you don't want anymore and quickly wrap it.

C) Give him the lovely big box of chocolates you'd been saving for yourself.

How did you score?

Mostly A

You are a fun-loving fairy and are enthusiastic about everything you do. You stay cheerful even when things go wrong. Your happy personality means you'll always have lots of fairy friends.

Mostly B

Oh dear! You can be a little bit of a thoughtless fairy sometimes. Try to be a bit more generous and join in more with all the other fairy activities. You'll have lots more fun!

Mostly C

You are everyone's favorite fairy friend. You are kind and considerate and always thinking of others. Give yourself a big pat on the back — the Fairy Queen would be proud of you!

✴ Autumn Nature-Spotting ✴

We're going nature-spotting in the countryside. We're hoping to see lots of exciting creatures! I'm taking some binoculars, and on the way Nettle is going to teach us the Fairy Country Code.

Hmm, gnawed bark — must have been a squirrel.

Wild animals are very shy and secretive. They'll often hide away when they see fairies coming. So, to spot them, the fairies will have to be very patient and quiet!

Gosh, three fox cubs!

I see two mice!

Me, too!

Nibbled seeds can mean that some mice have been feeding close by. Lavender has spotted something in the grass.

Squeak!

Bluebell has found a fox's den under a tree. She is being as silent as she can while she watches excitedly to see if any baby foxes come out to play.

I've just come across this tuft of animal hair caught on a fence. I think it has come from a sheep.

Look, Blossom! A deer!

Look, Thumper! A fairy!

This time we're the ones being followed!

A good way of tracking animals is by looking for their footprints in the earth. Here are some bird tracks — I wonder what they'll lead us to. . . .

★ Butterfly Mobile ★

Caw! Would you make a bird mobile next, Blossom?

Use the beautiful Fairyland butterfly stickers to make a mobile just like this!

You will need: Two sticks from the garden or park (about 7 inches long) 36 inches (1 yard) length of narrow ribbon ⋆ Cotton thread ⋆ Fairyland stickers

1. Tie one end of the ribbon to the middle of the longer stick. Then tie the shorter stick halfway along the ribbon. The loose end of ribbon is for hanging up the mobile.

2. Take the butterfly stickers and match them back-to-back, locking one end of the cotton thread in between each pair. Cut the cotton to about 6 inches in length.

3. Tie the other end of each cotton thread to the sticks, as shown.

4. Ask an adult to tie your mobile up somewhere safely.

I've hung my mobile by the window.

They're shimmering, Blossom!

Look! There's one just like me!

★ Blossom Goes Camping ★

Blossom is excited. She and her friends are going camping in Fairyland woods. They've packed their backpacks — let's hope they haven't forgotten anything important!

Hmm, I wonder what this tastes like!

Hurrah — we're off!

The fairies have walked deep into the woods. Hightail flies overhead to watch for danger.

Caw!

Here's the campsite!

Oh, at last!

Whoops!

Trust Hollyhock!

Blossom and her friends are all sharing a big tent they have made themselves.

What a lovely place!

Oh, no! I've forgotten my sleeping bag.

Never mind!

There's so much to be done before nightfall.

Everything is unpacked, and all the jobs are done. Supper is ready too!

It's getting dark now, and the stars are twinkling overhead in the night sky.

After supper everyone sings the secret fairy camp song, to the tune of *"For He's a Jolly Good Fellow."*

It's been a wonderful day, and now it's time for bed. No one feels the least bit sleepy, so Blossom tells one of her special bedtime stories. Turn the page to hear it, too.

⋆ Snowdrop's Sale ⋆

Once upon a time there was a fairy called Snowdrop. Snowdrop lived in a wood on the far side of Fairyland. She loved her quiet house, which was in the hollow of a large apple tree. There was an empty tree house in the branches, and beneath the tree's roots was an old badger burrow. In spring this was smothered in bright yellow crocuses.

Snowdrop's home was rather big for one fairy — but Snowdrop thought it was just perfect. However, there was another problem. Very few fairies lived nearby. Poor Snowdrop sometimes got very lonely.

"If only I had some neighbors close by," Snowdrop sighed to herself one morning. "Perhaps I should move to a busier part of Fairyland."

The thought of leaving her apple tree standing empty was very sad, but she decided she must move. So she wrote out a huge "For Sale" sign and hung it from the branches of her apple tree. Then she set off toward the center of Fairyland to see if she could find herself somewhere new to live.

Snowdrop spent a busy morning flying around,

searching for a suitable house. There was nothing she liked at all, so she decided to try again after lunch. But as she arrived back home, she had a surprise waiting for her. Sitting on her doorstep were two fairies.

"Hello." The fairies smiled at Snowdrop. "We were flying past when we spotted your "For Sale" sign. We're looking for a new home, and this apple tree looks lovely!"

Snowdrop was delighted. "Come inside and look around," she said, inviting them in.

The two fairies, called Posie and Rosie, were shown all over Snowdrop's tree hollow. When the tour had finished, they both looked a little embarrassed.

"We really only wanted to move into the empty tree house above," Rosie said.

"Yes," added Posie. "We forgot to explain. It has a lovely view up there."

"Oh, sorry!" Snowdrop replied, feeling disappointed. "What a shame."

No sooner had Rosie and Posie waved good-bye, than there was another rat-a-tat-tat on the front door. Snowdrop answered it to find another smiling fairy.

"I'm Forget-me-not," said the fairy cheerily. "I noticed your 'For Sale' sign and rushed over. This place is just what I've been looking for!"

Happily, Snowdrop showed Forget-me-not all around her home.

"It's very nice," Forget-me-not said. "But I wanted to make my home in the empty badger burrow. Badger burrows are so cozy," she added. Snowdrop was upset that no one seemed interested in her lovely home. She was already feeling fed up with the whole idea of moving.

It was too late to go house-hunting that afternoon, so Snowdrop baked some fairy cakes instead. She was just taking them out of the oven when another visitor arrived. This time it was a little fairy called Daisy, who had seen the "For Sale" sign.

"You do want a home in the tree's hollow?" Snowdrop checked with her. "Not in the branches or under the roots?"

Daisy assured Snowdrop she wanted a tree hollow, so Snowdrop invited her in. But although Daisy loved the house, she said it was far too big and lonely for her.

"It is large," Snowdrop agreed sadly, wondering if she would ever find someone who would like to live in her home. "The hollow is really meant for two fairies."

Then, all of a sudden, Snowdrop had a wonderful idea. "Wait here," she told Daisy. "Don't move! I'm off to find Rosie, Posie, and Forget-me-not!"

Fortunately Snowdrop found them all looking at houses quite nearby. Together they returned to Daisy in the hollow, feeling quite puzzled.

"I only wanted to move so I could meet new friends," Snowdrop explained. "Now I've thought of a way I can have friends close by — without moving!"

Snowdrop's plan was that Rosie and Posie should move into the empty tree house, and Forget-me-not could live inside the old badger burrow. Both houses had been empty for years and years.

"What about me?" piped up Daisy.

"The hollow is meant for two fairies," Snowdrop said excitedly. "Would you like to share the hollow with me? We could be great friends!"

A great cheer went up. It was the perfect solution.

"Now everyone's happy!" laughed Snowdrop, as she handed around a plateful of her delicious fairy cakes. She was so pleased. Not only could she stay in her lovely home — but she now had plenty of new friends around, too!

✳ What Fairy Job Would You Do? ✳

Would you prefer to work in Fairyland's perfume factory or become a fashion fairy? Do my quiz and find out what fairy job would most suit you. On a piece of paper, write down each answer you would choose.

1. It's a lovely sunny day. Would you most like to:

A) Meet your friends for a great picnic in Fairyland woods.

B) Go shopping and treat yourself to some new glittery jewelry.

C) Have fun taking the baby fairies swimming in the stream.

2. Your best friend asks you to help out at her little sister's birthday party. Do you:

A) Spend all day cooking up some delicious party treats.

B) Make lots of pretty pins and rings for the young fairies to win as prizes.

C) Help with the party games and make sure everyone's having fun.

3. You've just gotten home from a lovely vacation at the seashore. What's the first thing you do?
A) Just relax — it's great to be in your own home again.
B) Read the fab fashion magazine that arrived while you were away!
C) Rush around to see your friends.

4. You spot a fairy trail in the woods and decide to follow it. Where do you hope it leads to?
A) Your dream cottage in the middle of an apple orchard.
B) A treasure chest hidden deep in the forest.
C) A secret hideout where your friends are waiting for you with a wonderful surprise!

5. You wake up to find Fairyland covered in deep snow. Do you:
A) Stay indoors — it looks freezing outside.
B) Dress up in your new snowsuit and go out sledding.
C) Organize a snowman-building competition!

How did you score?

Mostly A
You are a home-loving fairy and love cooking. You would enjoy working in the palace kitchens or growing fruit and vegetables in the Fairy Queen's garden.

Mostly B
You love pretty trinkets and wearing the latest fairy fashions. A job making jewelry and gorgeous clothes with the fashion fairies would suit you perfectly.

Mostly C
You like being with fairies of all ages and love meeting new friends. You'd make a wonderful teacher at the Fairyland school, or you might enjoy a job as a mail fairy.

Autumn and Winter Fashion Fun

It's getting cold again in Fairyland, and an exciting new fashion season has begun! My Boutique is full of all the latest fairy clothes and accessories.

I'm decorating my tiaras with jewels.

Caw!

Help, these boots are stuck!

Gift Wrapping Service

★ Glitter Snowstorm ★

I've chosen a jolly Santa Claus and reindeer toy for my snowstorm — it looks really Christmassy. You could use a pretty toy fairy!

You will need: A clear glass food jar with a screw-on lid (choose a short, fat jar with a nice lid) ＊ White modeling clay ＊ A plastic toy or Christmas novelty Glycerine (to slow the fall of the glitter) ＊ Silver glitter ＊ Blue food coloring

1. Wash the jar thoroughly and remove any labels. Make sure the jar is airtight.

Wheee!

2. Cover the inside of the lid with a mound of modeling clay to look like snow.

Your toy should be no bigger than the jar!

3. Push the toy or Christmas decoration firmly into the modeling clay and mold the clay around the toy to help keep it in place.

4. Check the instructions on the glycerine bottle and half fill your jar with glycerine. Pour in water until the jar is three-quarters full. Add a tablespoon of glitter and a few drops of the food coloring.

5. Carefully lower the lid onto the jar. The liquid will rise up.

6. If the liquid doesn't fill the jar completely, add a little more water. Then ask an adult to screw the lid on tightly.

Always use things that water won't spoil!

Wow!

So sparkly!

7. Give the jar a good shake and turn the jar upside down. Watch the glitter fall like sparkling snow!

✦ First Snow in Fairyland ✦

One morning the fairies woke to find Fairyland covered in deep snow. Winter had arrived!

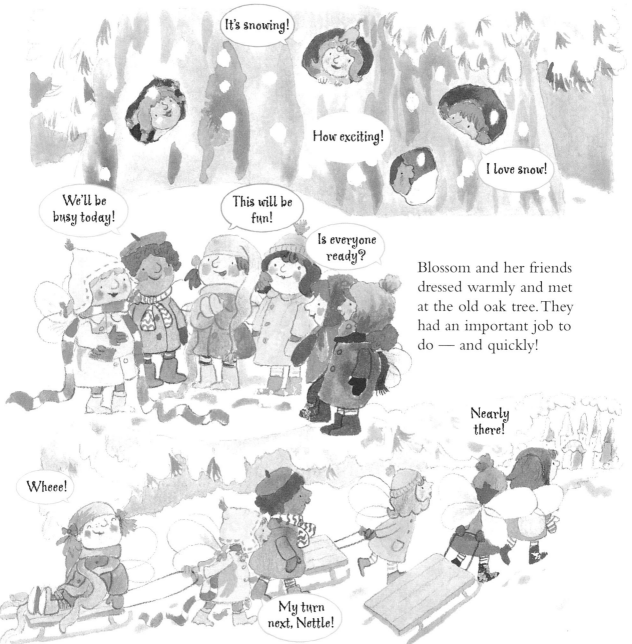

Blossom and her friends dressed warmly and met at the old oak tree. They had an important job to do — and quickly!

The fairies like to check that the animals and birds are ready for the winter. Snow causes all sorts of problems for the fairies' animal friends. First the fairies headed for the palace.

Blossom and Lavender piled their sleigh high with food from the royal kitchens.

The squirrels should love those acorns.

That bread is for the birds, Nettle!

Yummy!

the Queen's shed

So soft and cozy!

Room for another!

Meanwhile Bluebell and the others collected bags of thistledown bedding.

Phew, this is heavy!

Missed!

Oops!

Once loaded up, everyone set off for Fairyland woods. It looked beautiful in the snow!

Three hungry squirrels raced out to meet the fairies. Blossom gave them some acorns.

Tasty!

Thanks!

Zzzz

I'll just tuck them in.

Poor things! You must be hungry.

Meanwhile Nettle was checking that all the dormice were safely asleep in their nests.

One dormouse wasn't ready at all! Nettle's woolly hat made a perfect instant nest!

Yawn!

That's better.

At Fairyland lake the ducks were starving! They ate all of the bread!

Quack!

Wheee!

Brrr, it's cold!

This will keep the wind out.

They looked inside the rabbit warrens. Many of them needed extra warm bedding.

Oh dear! One of the rabbit holes looked very drafty!

My mittens make great bird feeders!

Snug!

You'll be warm now.

The birds *were* pleased! They fluttered down to eat the seeds and nuts.

Finally all the creatures had been taken care of. Happily the fairies headed back through the snow.

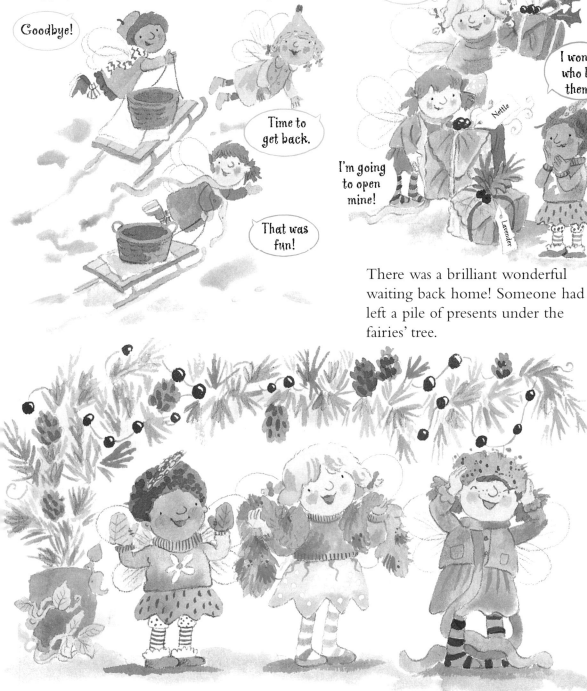

There was a brilliant wonderful waiting back home! Someone had left a pile of presents under the fairies' tree.

They were great "thank you" gifts from the woodland creatures — and were exactly what everyone needed! Now no one will be cold this winter!

Trust me! I've lost one of my gloves. Can you spot it anywhere?

A very Merry Christmas to all Fairies!

How many snowmen can you find hidden in the picture?

Let's gather together all the wrapping paper!

Recycling

Four friendly creatures are hiding in the pile of wrapping paper. Can you tell who they are?

Which balloon is Bluebell holding?

Answers
The identical Santa biscuits are numbers 2 and 6. Nettle has eaten five cakes. The creatures in the wrapping paper are ladybug, caterpillar, bee, and spider. Bluebell has a yellow balloon, and there are eight snowmen.

Fairy Washday

Many people believe that fairies don't like to get wet, but Blossom and her friends love to have a dip in a leaf pond. The only problem they have is afterward — sorting out which clothes belong to which fairy! Can you help?

Ⓐ

Ⓑ

Ⓒ Ⓓ

Ⓔ

Oh, which socks are mine?

Ⓘ